ADVENTURE HUNTERS

Thrilling Tales

Edited By Jenni Harrison

First published in Great Britain in 2022 by:

Young Writers
Remus House
Coltsfoot Drive
Peterborough
PE2 9BF
Telephone: 01733 890066
Website: www.youngwriters.co.uk

Book Design by Ashley Janson

Softback ISBN 978-1-80015-858-0

Printed and bound in the UK by BookPrintingUK
Website: www.bookprintinguk.com
YB0498W

FOREWORD

Are you searching for adventure? Then come right this way – fun and daring deeds await! It's very simple, all you have to do is turn the page and you'll be transported into a wealth of amazing adventure stories.

Is it magic? Is it a trick? No! It's all down to the skill and imagination of primary school pupils from around the country. For our latest competition Adventure Hunters, we gave them the task of writing a story on any topic, and to do it in just 100 words! I think you'll agree they've achieved that brilliantly – this book is jam-packed with exciting and thrilling tales.

These young authors have brought their ideas to life using only their words. This is the power of creativity and it gives us life too! Here at Young Writers we want to pass our love of the written word onto the next generation and what better way to do that than to celebrate their writing by publishing it in a book!

It sets their work free from homework books and notepads and puts it where it deserves to be – out in the world and preserved forever! Each awesome author in this book should be super proud of themselves, and now they've got proof of their ideas and their creativity in black and white, to look back on in years to come!

We hope you enjoy this book as much as we have! Now it's time to let imagination take control, so read on...

CONTENTS

Lakes Primary School, Redcar

THE
STORIES

The Treasure Hunt

"I've found the treasure map," cried Sam.

"Have you actually?" shouted Fred. "If you have let's go and find it."

They went across fields, roads and then they found a deep, dark cave.

"I'm not going in there," said Sam.

"Come on it will be fine," replied Fred. Then they went into the huge dark cave. There were a lot of ways they could go.

"Let's go this way," said Fred. Then they found a huge golden box of treasure.

"It is all mine," said Sam, "because I found the map."

"That's not fair," Fred said. "Let's go this way."

Hussain Rizwan (10)

All Saints' CE (A) Primary School, Peterborough

Saviours Of Our World

"Really!? You think we can save the world from climate change in a month?" shouted Laura.
"Well, we can try," exclaimed Ben.
"You do know it will take a whole year for the government to save climate change and help the world, Ben," said Laura.
But all of a sudden the lights in the house switched off and a voice murmured, "You can do it, save the world."
"What was that?" they both whispered.
"I don't know," Laura said quietly and carefully as they moved to the corner, but lurking out of the shadows was a great, big, furry monster...

Habibah Javed (10)
All Saints' CE (A) Primary School, Peterborough

The Truth About Mars

As I walked onto the extraordinary planet, Mars, I talked to my fellow comrades,
"Julian, keep an eye out for her," but knowing Julian, he'd get lost in five minutes! "We came here on a mission and now we're going to succeed!"
"Umm... Captain, you might want to see this." I marched over to him, I saw an almost unconscious human body! We lifted her.
"Where am I!?" screamed the lady, but before Julian could explain she roared in anger, "Who am I?" However, I was too distracted because of a shiny, gold box beneath her. I opened it up...

Habibah Hussain (10)

All Saints' CE (A) Primary School, Peterborough

The Mask Does All

They spawned without any notice whatsoever, George and Clay had to fight against mobs; it was a trouble getting into the portal that would lead them to the Ender dragon. Its eyes glowed and its roars were loud. They could end the whole thing. George fired arrows to the spawners, Clay had his sword out, the dragon came! Almost dead, George fired while Clay stabbed the dragon! One more stab and the end, George lept for it, it happened! Finally, it was over.
"Good job!" Clay said.
"Thanks, we did together!" George replied, this was usual for them.

Zainab Tariq (11)
All Saints' CE (A) Primary School, Peterborough

Cave Of Wonders!

I stumbled through the pitch-black cave. Not knowing where I was, I tripped over the rocks, which made it hard in the darkness, and fell onto my face. I was sweating, water dripped from my forehead, what had I done? Terrified, I walked on but something instantly stopped me. "A wall," I murmured to myself. Like a blind bat, I felt for a hole to crawl through, my hand slipped down. A door. The door creaked open, millions of glistening jewels fascinated me. I had never seen it before. "Argh!" someone screamed. Who was it...?

Chloe Graham (10)

All Saints' CE (A) Primary School, Peterborough

Big Mac And The Metal Monkey

Deep in the dark, misty jungle lay a sleeping, metal monkey and a brave heroic boy: Big Mac. One afternoon, Big Mac became lost in the dense jungle. He turned left then right, then right again but couldn't find his way out. Unexpectedly, he stumbled and knocked his head against something that looked like a rock. Out of nowhere a giant metal monkey arose from his slumber and tried to slash Big Mac with his metal banana. As he dived to the side he spotted a glamorous looking sword sticking out of the monkey's back; but it was too late...

Thomas Gray (10)

All Saints' CE (A) Primary School, Peterborough

The Dark Creature

As I moved stealthily I suddenly heard a loud snap, but then Sherlock realised he'd stepped on a twig. We had been travelling for ages but we needed to find the creature the creepy old man told us about, he had given me a Sherlock sword and said, "Defeat a monster for me in the forest and I'll make you rich." We found a trail of something or someone with extremely large footsteps. But then realised it was an overweight gorilla. We really needed the money because we were both poor, but had the gloomy old man lied to us...?

Muhammad Warfan Ahmad (10)
All Saints' CE (A) Primary School, Peterborough

The Crystal Key

Bang! Crash! Boom! They were on my back. Out of breath, I looked for a place to hide. I thought to myself, *I have to find the key.* I could hear the dogs ferociously barking. Terrified, I looked behind me. I knew I was near to my destination - the key. Racing over the crooked unstable bridge, I saw the crystal-covered key. Part of me was happy knowing I was there, but part of me was scared knowing that the crystal key guards might still be here! Suddenly, I heard footsteps. I looked around and saw the guards right there...

Gideon Cole (10)

All Saints' CE (A) Primary School, Peterborough

Star Treasure

The map had led me here. I had gone through the Sunset Jungle and the Cloudy Wastelands to get here, to the Moonlight Cavern. As I stepped forward I slipped and slid down the cave until I crashed into a wall! When I got up, luckily I was not injured, I discovered that there were two star shapes carved into the wall. I reached into my bag; the stars were glowing brighter than before! I pushed the stars into place... and there it was, the treasure. With the key weighing down I took it off and slowly opened the chest...

Julia Nanji (10)
All Saints' CE (A) Primary School, Peterborough

Save A Friend

It was when I went in that I saw my friend with a witch that was holding her. I hid so the witch didn't see me. I stayed there and waited. When she was gone I went to where the witch went and put my friend in a room. So I went to the door and said, "Friend?"
She said, "Yes."
I said, "Where's the key?"
And she said, "It's in his room." There he was sleeping so I went and took the key. So I went to her and opened the door. We went home.

Yasmin Corte Real Furtado (11)
All Saints' CE (A) Primary School, Peterborough

Joe's Final Mission

Joe is relaxing at home when he gets a text from his friend saying he needs to be saved in the Caribbean, so he gets up to save him. He's in a plane going to the Caribbean. He is hanging above a lava pit whilst Joe is trying to save him. Joe is a master at everything but his enemy Mama is there to stop him. He is dodging hits left and right and manages to escape to his friend Max and with perfect devotion saves him from falling. Finally, they take down Mama and they go to their home.

Aryaan Hussain (10)
All Saints' CE (A) Primary School, Peterborough

The King Of Pirates

When I was young, I had the power to breathe underwater, but I didn't know how to control it. I wanted to find a treasure that makes you the king of pirates. So I went to find it (I had a rough idea because of a treasure map I found) and I looked everywhere for it. Then I decided to look underwater. So after a few hours, I thought I found it, but it was just gold. I started getting kind of happy, but I kicked the sand and then my foot hurt, so I dug, and found the treasure!

Salmaan Asaf (10)
All Saints' CE (A) Primary School, Peterborough

The Forest

"Where are we?" asked Ava.

"It says here, we have to find the missing piece!"

"Missing piece!" came a voice from behind. "I'm Claire, you can come to my house to stay." We all went to the house, shut the door and sat down. I looked around. Everything linked to the missing piece!

"You're it!" I said.

"What do you mean?"

"You're the missing piece!"

"Really! Is she really?" said Ava curiously.

"Yes! How many times!" I replied. "If you come with us, we could save the forest!" I said.

"Well, what are we waiting for? Let's go!" said Claire.

River Kaur Simmonds (10)

Buckingham Park CE Primary School, Buckingham Park

The Cave

Crumble! The stones crumbled underfoot as I ran for shelter. It was raining. It was dark and cold.
"I can see it!" I screamed. "I can see shelter," I continued.
"Where?" said Tom.
"Over there!" I pointed. It was warm. "Let's discover this place," I said.
"Yeah that's a good idea." We walked around the cave and saw some peculiar pictures on the wall. One of the pictures said, 'You are the one'. *I wonder who that might be,* I thought. *Who is the one?*
"Tom I found something, it's a few pictures."
"I wonder who the one is?"

Ivan Jojo Dadzie (10)
Buckingham Park CE Primary School, Buckingham Park

The Kidnapper

We had been trapped in a shed for a day or two and we found that our kidnapper goes for one hour.

"We could escape when they go," I said.

"I'm scared," whimpered Elise.

Charlotte started to look under all the furniture, she found a key. "I found a key!" she screamed.

"Unlock me first please the handcuffs are rubbing on my cut!" yelled Elise.

After a while, we found a keycard. It opened a door. *Boom! Beep!* The light turned off.

"Argh! We're gonna die!" yelled Elise.

The door was an escape. It turned dark. We heard a scream.

Natalia Pietrala (10)

Buckingham Park CE Primary School, Buckingham Park

The Slayer

Creak! Eugene opened the graveyard's gates to stop Einstein, he was attempting to bring back the dead.
"Stop!" Eugene screamed. He always carried a pocket knife. He knew one day he would need it. Luckily it was misty so Eugene ducked, dived, and rolled towards him. Einstein was starting to pick up the pace while digging. So as Eugene was running he heard a scream, it was Einstein. A cluster of spiders crawled out. Eugene knew it was his chance. He sprinted toward the figure, he jumped and stabbed him with his red knife and Einstein was gone. *Squelch!* Eww!

Joseph Hawkins (11)
Buckingham Park CE Primary School, Buckingham Park

Saving The World

Crash! The world-o-meter was failing and quick. We tried to get everyone off Earth but there were some that refused and remained, but me and Sadey couldn't worry about them now, we had to focus on evacuating the few that did believe our statement.
"What about my son? I live on Boulevard Lane!" cried a woman. Me and Sadey glanced at each other. Then I leapt out the spacecraft and ran.
"Claire!" said a voice behind me. The boy was sitting on his bed, I grabbed him and I glanced at my watch. Three seconds left... One! Two! Three! *Boom!*

Claire Robertson (10)
Buckingham Park CE Primary School, Buckingham Park

The Daunting Desert

Clash! The tunnel worm descended beneath me. Its venomous spines threatened my life as I crouched down close to the beast's head, drew out my short blade and stabbed at the worm's plates. My ears were ringing with the sound of failure as the knife bounced off the monster's cranium.
"Hey, Jack!" I shouted at the boy that was chasing chickens. "Pass me the thing!" I shrieked. Of course I didn't trust him with his butter fingers but it was all I had got. The vial of poison that he threw was on the knife and, obviously, the worm died.

Gabriel Repton (11)
Buckingham Park CE Primary School, Buckingham Park

The Waterfall

Splash! The water flowed beneath my feet. My mum stepped closer. *Crash*. My mum fell... Shocked, I stood frozen. What do I do? I looked over the edge. My mum was still alive. Hesitantly, I searched for a place to jump from. Finally, I built up the courage to jump. I dived screaming at the top of my lungs. *Bang!* The impact slowed me down. My mum was going under. I needed to pick up the pace. Finally, I reached her. As we swam to safety, I asked my mum to never take me here again. She promised. Never again.

Riley Baxter (10)
Buckingham Park CE Primary School, Buckingham Park

Defeating The Giant

It was a race against time and that giant. My shoes had burned away. The soles of my feet scorched with every step up the quaking volcano. The existence of the human race depended on me. I had to destroy the human guzzling giant. For my plan to work, I had to win the dash to the top. The giant's feet were stomping closer. Fiery liquid spat and spewed over my head. I reached the peak. I turned to look back. The giant lunged at me, I ducked, dived and rolled. *Splash!* Yes, I had saved the world. I'm victorious.

Paras Singh (10)

Buckingham Park CE Primary School, Buckingham Park

The Special Fruit

I was running the fastest I ever had. A hungry cheetah was chasing me. Suddenly, everything but me had frozen. I had to save the animals. I ran, panted and leapt straight into a cave. Suddenly! The cheetah was back and he charged straight at me. I thought to myself, *how did he unfreeze?* Then there it was, the special fruit I needed to save the animals. I took a bite and in an instant, I saved the animals. Now all I had to do was save myself from the hungry cheetah, but how? Then a trapdoor! I was safe!

Elise Breith (11)
Buckingham Park CE Primary School, Buckingham Park

The Magic Potion

Crunch. My cat started meowing, I looked around and saw a key. I picked it up and noticed this was the one I'd been looking for. I looked on my digital map. *Beep! Beep!* My map said I was standing on it but I couldn't see anything. My cat stepped on a button and I felt I was getting higher. Then I grabbed my cat, jumped off the cabin and crouched down. The cabin was arising from the ground. I put the key in the door and opened it. In the cabin was the potion that could save the world.

Effie Dean (10)
Buckingham Park CE Primary School, Buckingham Park

The Beast

The existence of the human race relied on me. I had to go in. I entered and a wave of hot air hit my already hot skin. I walked a little further and that's when I saw it. The beast. I instantly yanked my sword and pointed it towards it. It tried to defend itself by throwing me against the wall. I pushed my feet off the wall and swung towards the beast. The sword went straight into the wall, the beast had teleported behind me. I rapidly turned around and threw my sword above it. Lava fell. *Squash.*

Ollie Saunders (11)
Buckingham Park CE Primary School, Buckingham Park

True Power

We were scared. Samantha had always been brave, but this was the first time I'd seen her cry. We were lost and the mansion was endless! We knew we were not alone; we were running and looking back. That was a mistake! Samantha fell headfirst into a glowing ball of light. As she lay twitching, I tried to call for help with my phone but there was no signal. I tried to help her but what I saw shocked me! As we both screamed for help a ball of fire shot out of her mouth! Something was wrong, very wrong...

Nehita Aigbogun (10)

Buckingham Park CE Primary School, Buckingham Park

Pirate Island

"James, come out of there," exclaimed Max. "It's very dangerous."

One hour earlier...

"This is very dark," shouted James. "It was supposed to be light. What's that sound?" murmured James. "It sounds like it's coming from over there."

"*Raaahh!*"

"What's that?" shouted James. "It sounds like it's a monster."

"It's Grim, the monster. I've taken the treasure," exclaimed Grim.

"I'll stop you," shouted James. They fought until James won and got the gold, glamorous treasure. He was going to return it to the King of Pirate Island.

"I declare you the new King of Pirate Island."

"That's amazing!" exclaimed James.

Cesare Pearce (9)

Crofton Junior School, Petts Wood

Krakshot's Escape!

Krakshot raced to the empty cell.
Bang! Bang!
"Mac, are you in there?" Krakshot cried. A deafening roar hit him hard, he saw a faint black shadow. It was Mac. Krakshot charged after Mac but he wasn't there. It was just an empty room...
Bang!
"Who's there?" Krakshot shouted aggressively.
"It is I, Goro the master of serpents," he hissed.
"Where's Mac?" Krakshot commanded.
"In my lair," he hissed.
Krakshot in anger swung his golden hammer. Goro was dead. Mac came running with a smile.
"Let's get you home safe shall we," Krakshot whispered.
"Yes!" Mac cried.

Nathan Evered (10)
Crofton Junior School, Petts Wood

The Siren Monster

"Every night, Siren Monster kills one person and eats them," whispered Saphira.

"It's night though," complained Jake.

"*Err-err!*" Siren Monster yelled.

Siren Monster had killed Saphira and Jake's parents and they wanted revenge. Jake crept forward. "Do you think behind a tree is a good hiding spot?" whispered Jake.

"He's coming closer," mumbled Saphira. Saphira always kept a knife on her so she leapt onto Siren Monster and cut one of his sirens off. Just then, Jake fainted.

Siren Monster was so tall. He grabbed Saphira and dropped her 100 metres. When she got dropped, she cut the Siren's head.

Delilah Mercer (8)

Crofton Junior School, Petts Wood

Zombie Squad

"Have you heard the news? There's zombies in town!" Zac asked.

"What!" Jasmine shouted.

"*Er*," Billy said.

"Stop!" Rohan shouted. "That's not going to stop us from getting the diamond to kill the zombies."
They were the Zombie Squad. They had been waiting for this moment for ten years straight.

"I am so, so scared," Zac shrieked.

Just then, a zombie came up to them and touched Zac, Jasmine, and Billy. Which meant that only Rohan was left.
He ran to his mum and dad - and they weren't there! So he ran so fast to his uncle's house...

Nathaniel Poole (9)
Crofton Junior School, Petts Wood

The Book Of Magic Portals

Jess and James, brother and sister, were trying to get back to London. "What do we do, Jess?" whispered James.
"Hmm," whispered Jess. "Well, there is something called the magic portal." So Jess and James started looking everywhere for it, since they were basically in the middle of nowhere. All of a sudden, Jess found a book. "This is the book of magic portals," claimed Jess.
They looked through the book of magic portals and found what they needed. "I've found it," screamed James. "Say, spells of the middle of nowhere." Well, James and Jess made it back to London!

Madeline Sinclair (9)
Crofton Junior School, Petts Wood

Shipwreck

Blood. A blurred vision. Sleek, grey shapes lurked underneath the unconscious bodies. A gloomy shadow swallowed up the murder. Thick, murky fog hid the deceased. One left. Crushed ribs, hardly breathing. The survivor. Daylight broke the soulless night. Open eyes. Heavy gasping. Still, little life. Ripped skin, shredded like paper. Unoticeably shifting in the gritty sand. Slowly getting to her feet, Swift painfully opened her eyes. Unsuccessfully ignoring the screaming pain in her muscles, she started walking along the beach. Even though she was gifted with coconuts and palm trees, she had no water. There was no chance of survival.

Natasha Hallworth (10)
Crofton Junior School, Petts Wood

The Mythical Forest

Poof! Bailey appeared in this magnificent forest and found a beautiful jewel. She picked it up and looked closely into it, a fairy appeared!
The beautiful fairy jumped into Bailey's hands and, before Bailey could blink, she flew onto the flowers. Her name was Rosie, she had glittery wings, a sparkly dress that looked like a pot of glitter. She took Bailey's hand and led her deeper into the forest and said, "I can turn this place into whatever you want it to be." Bailey wanted lots of pink prettiness and glittery magical flowers.
Boom! The magical forest changed.

Bailey Manning (10)
Crofton Junior School, Petts Wood

Scorch's Tale

Scorch ruffled his claws. "Today it might happen." He outstretched his wings and took off into the sky. By the time the other firedragons had woken up, he had circled the island twelve times.
"No seadragons today then." Something glistened in the corner of his eye. "What's that?" He landed. It was the Queen's Medallion. When the dragons of the prophecy were alive, they gave it to the seadragons. He shot off into the sky to go to the seadragon palace. He gave it to the seadragons. "Peace at last," said Scorch. He returned home. War was finally over!

Ben Mercer (11)
Crofton Junior School, Petts Wood

The Astrologer

Once in space, there was someone called Alex, they were resting. It was a normal day, his alarm caught his attention. He pressed a button and a robot voice said, "The king of Pluto came to attack the zodiacs, we need your hel-" The alarm just died. Alex was the protector of the zodiacs. Alex went into a spaceship. "Give our zodiacs back."
"You kicked me out of the solar system."
"I don't want to do this." Alex stabbed him repeatedly. Calmly, Alex returned the zodiacs as if nothing had happened. That's how Alec saved the zodiacs and the universe.

Lidia Pikul (11)
Crofton Junior School, Petts Wood

A Battle Of Aliens

The two aliens circled each other, watching, waiting. They both wanted the Gem of Power, they had agreed that the winner would receive it. It was what every alien wanted, the gemstone of infinite possibility. Cannonrover curled into a ball and rolled, full speed, at Lavatongue. But, at the last moment, Lavatongue bounced upward and slammed a flaming fist into Cannonrover's hide. He screeched in pain and sent razor-sharp shards of metal towards his enemy. They were perfectly aimed but passed straight through him. He had conjured a mirage from the heat! So where was the real Lavatongue? Who knows?

Thomas Whitting (9)
Crofton Junior School, Petts Wood

The Map

As I galloped on my horse, (named Smartie) I saw a group of villagers crowded around something. I came to a halt, then asked, "What's going on?"
They said, "We have a map but don't know what it means."
I grabbed the map. "I'll help you." I set off galloping. I finally arrived. A witch's hut. She did it! She warned me about something. I didn't listen. I galloped back. Then told them what the map meant. Then, suddenly, there were heavy footsteps. It must have been the thing she warned me about. Everyone was confused and started to run.

Ellana Marshall (11)
Crofton Junior School, Petts Wood

Writho The Coiled Horror

In the blazing desert, George's clan cruised to find a bearable place to inhabit. But abruptly, the sand trembled. A vast snake shot out and people ran in terror. But obviously George was valiant. He raised his sword and shield and charged. He dodged the mighty beast's fangs and swung his sword at the creature's underside, creating a bloody wound. It roared in fury, and slithered towards George, and faster than even him, its tail whipped around him! He was being choked to death! But suddenly, Manu pounced from behind, and he sliced the creature in half! Saved! For now...

George Munton (9)
Crofton Junior School, Petts Wood

Trying To Reach Valhalla

Bjorn stepped outside his longhouse and stretched his legs. "*Argh!*" yelled Bjorn. He set off, determined to get to Valhalla. It was a Viking's dream to go to Valhalla. He set off at a quick pace toward the forest, which was behind his longhouse. Suddenly, he heard cries of terror coming from south of the dense, green forest. Suddenly, a huge monster crawled through the trees. *That must be what is making the noise*, thought Bjorn. He quickly rushed to kill the monster. But then the monster ate him. Bjorn was happy that he'd reached Valhalla at last.

Rohan Akkineni (8)
Crofton Junior School, Petts Wood

The Shadow Wolf

The jungle was dark. Smoke suddenly reached my nostrils, and I turned towards it. In the distance, flames were leaping into the air and I knew I had to get out of here. My heart sank. I didn't complete my quest to find the Shadow Wolf, but my life was more important. Too late. Flames surrounded me, choking my lungs, when a deafening *crack!* pierced through the air. Immediately, the flames retreated several metres and a ghostly wolf appeared, floating majestically in the air. Its paw touched me and pulled me from the flames. We landed, and *crack!* It disappeared.

Jacky Zheng (11)
Crofton Junior School, Petts Wood

Frankie's Wonderful Adventures

Once upon a time, there lived a girl named Frankie, she lived in New York. Frankie had a dream to explore the rainforest when she turns fifteen. Frankie is turning fifteen tomorrow so she is going to the rainforest.
Frankie was now on the beautiful, magnificent plane. She arrived at the rainforest and was so excited exploring, the plane left without her!
Frankie saw something glistening in the water. She dived in and what she didn't realise was that it was her glistening in the water. Once she was inside the lake she turned into a beautiful, magnificent pink mermaid.

Aimee Morgan (10)
Crofton Junior School, Petts Wood

A Lost Girl Stuck In The Middle Of The Ocean!

The parents couldn't see their young daughter Roze! She had been viciously swept into the deep dark terrifying ocean. Roze's parents were terrified, worried and screaming. They called the rescue team for help, the brave courageous rescue team got into a shiny light blue speedboat that was as fast as a cheetah chasing its prey. Roze was being aided by a furious, frightening shark. One of the confident rescuers scared the shark by punching it in the gills but then the other members threw an inflatable hoop and pulled Roze safely onto the boat. The parents were ecstatic!

Brooklyn Wyatt (8)
Crofton Junior School, Petts Wood

Agent R And The Tale Of A Rather Cracked Egg

In the heart of the jungle, where sneaky snakes are, Agent R isn't too far. Hired by EGG (Electronic Gigatron Group) she's on a mission to recover an unknown item. *Whirr!* The helicopter lands. Over comms: "Retrieve the item and meet at the rendevous point."

Agent R swooped through the trees, over the slimy snakes. She knew something was suspicious, she came in for a closer look and to her surprise, there was a hollow volcano and it had a chest in the middle. She carefully extracted the item and left. Back at EGG HQ, she returned it.

Alex Ranasinghe (10)

Crofton Junior School, Petts Wood

Death

"Lucy!" I yelled. My voice was hoarse with calling out. Screaming in the thick black smoke and trying to get a clear view of the volcano. I couldn't believe she'd ventured down there alone. It's one thing to run away, another to go into an active volcano. Suddenly, I was deafened by the shrill scream of the helicopter as it spiralled downwards and I jumped... Then it came. A stabbing pain as a jagged rock tore my skin. I howled in agony. Falling, falling while the blistering heat came closer. The last thing I heard was a piercing scream. Lucy...

Aaryan Sood (10)
Crofton Junior School, Petts Wood

Out Of This World

I escaped, but did I get away? Where am I? Maybe an unearthly, unknown forest. I'd made very bad mistakes. I went deeper and looked at my watch. The hands were flickering all over the place. The darkness was nigh, it was misty. I saw something in the distance. It was black, I ran towards it. It was a gate. I ran through the nettles and through the gate, the colour was red now.
"Bob! Eat your dinner before you go on the virtual reality headset!" a female voice shouted. "Come, now!"
"Okay!" said I, and fell down the stairs.

Bertie Morrison (9)
Crofton Junior School, Petts Wood

Zombie Town

I had a mission to protect Zombie Town. Suddenly, a zombie scared my girlfriend and she jumped into my arms. "I've got you, Olivia. No one will hurt you my-"
"Don't you dare say girlfriend. For the last time Fred. I'm not your girlfriend!" shouted Olivia. Then humans came. We fought and fought until sunset when it was a disaster.
The next day, we had an idea to put cannons in the buildings. Then they came again. We were ready. It worked. So Olivia gave me an amazing kiss. This time, we actually started dating. Finally!

Poppy Zincke (11)
Crofton Junior School, Petts Wood

The Missing Friend

In the sombre forest, Peyton and Jess ventured into the abandoned forest to find their missing friend, Kayla. It was a week since she was missing. They had gathered the gear and set off. It was eerie, leaves crunching. Was someone following them? They ignored the mysterious sounds and carried on. Many more sounds, like breathing and scuffing boots, followed them. They started to run. In the distance, a cage was seen, with someone in it. Could that be Kayla? They got closer, it was her! They got her out. But Zach came. Police arrested him. He was gone, finally!

Jessica Green (11)
Crofton Junior School, Petts Wood

The Great Adventure

In this abandoned school, there were three young children, Sid, Sam and Aiden that all used to go to the school, until there was an evacuation and the school closed down. These three children all wanted to find out why, so they went on a mystery adventure. One of them went missing... so the others explored the school, everything appeared to be normal until... They heard footsteps, so quickly found somewhere safe to hide, that's when they found their friend tied to a chair, Liam, their old friend, was holding a gun to his head. What will happen next?.....

Sidney Green Paget (10)
Crofton Junior School, Petts Wood

The Monster...

We'd been walking for days, and I was beginning to feel so creeped out since we were trudging through a filthy, derelict wasteland. I told Jez that we should turn back, but he was so determined to find this treasure that probably wasn't even real! So we carried on, night pouring in and surrounding us in a black sea of darkness. I kept seeing faces staring at us. I definitely heard something, then, looking behind me, I saw the most blood-curdling thing. Thick, red pools of blood for eyes, a mouth stretched into a petrifying grin, reaching towards us.

Sophie Hunt (11)
Crofton Junior School, Petts Wood

The Escape

I've been here for twenty-seven torturous years. Time to escape. According to plan, I tiptoed through the corridor and then crawled through an air vent. After scrambling through the ant-sized vent, I found myself in a long, concrete tunnel. A sixth sense told me that it was the way. Finally, I'd be free from this prison! Suddenly, the alarm went off! Oh no! I sprinted at the speed of light towards the light at the end. The cops were behind me. "Stop!" a voice bellowed. Something hit me. My eyes slowly shut at the end. Was I free?

William Ng (10)
Crofton Junior School, Petts Wood

Sacrifice

Stara stared with the rope clutched in her hand. Deathshadow flew beneath her, dodging bombs as they fell. Ash flew as it always did. It was now or never. Stara slid down the rope with bombs falling beside her, Deathshadow beneath her. She slid inside, away from the fools trying to enter at the door. Deathshadow smashed another door when landing. Stara rushed through the hole, blown inside by a bomb. She punched a box open and pulled out a scroll. Knife ready. She got it and now it was gone. So was she.
Deathshadow protected her grave. Sacrifice.

Charlotte Jessop (11)
Crofton Junior School, Petts Wood

The Dream

It was an ordinary day. We were going to the beach. Then she came. Her name was Doctor Who.
"Hi," she said. I didn't know what to do.
She opened her box thing, it was actually called a TARDIS. It was massive inside. Then I heard a noise, it was an alien. It wasn't an ordinary alien.
"What do you want?" she said.
"I want to take over the planet," it said.
I was so scared. *What is going to happen?* I thought, so I ran into the TARDIS. Then I woke up, it was a dream. *Phew*, I thought.

Imogen Ward (11)
Crofton Junior School, Petts Wood

The Kidnapping

Planet Nowhere, a planet where you fight to survive. Ruled by the king, whose son, sadly, was kidnapped. After that day, the king set out to find his son, his only clue being he was in the quantonium system.
Sam had been kidnapped and put in an arena where they would fight until they died. Sam was fighting, his next opponent was his father. As Sam had been kidnapped when he was very young, he didn't recognise his father and his father did not recognise his son. They fought and fought and in the end, they tragically died together fighting.

Samuel Clinkscales (11)
Crofton Junior School, Petts Wood

The Evil Sorcerer

As I opened my eyes I noticed I was in the school hospital. I saw my brother Jacob staring at me. We'd failed to defeat our enemy the evil sorcerer and now we'd have to explain. Luckily, Hecole (our mother) wasn't mad, so after explaining, we planned to defeat her eventually, it meant leaving demigod school again. A bit later we left.
Upon our arrival, we went inside and I paralyzed her whilst Jacob stabbed her. Finally, after years, we'd killed her. She was dead. A hole opened. She fell straight down, never to be seen again.

Maggie Wall (10)
Crofton Junior School, Petts Wood

Invaders

As the army rode through the forest, they spotted the top of a house and stopped. They then put on their armour and grabbed swords and shields. Soon they charged at the guards and the village. Erick led the charge because he was the King. Many on each side died but Erick's army outnumbered the guards. Erick knew more guards would arrive, and his army was tired, so he retreated. When they were ready, they rode toward the village and faced another battle. But rode on into the village and rode around killing everyone. So soon, everyone was dead.

Harrison McCullagh (8)
Crofton Junior School, Petts Wood

Fantasy FC Stadium

"Here it is," said Bob to Jeff. Jeff hadn't believed that Bob had found an abandoned stadium or that they had to win a game for it to be renovated and reopened. It's going to be Football Fantasy FC vs The Best Team In The World FC. As they walked into the stadium they felt a pump of adrenaline run through their bodies. Football Fantasy FC got into their positions. It was a tense game throughout. It came down to the final shot. Jeff passed to Bob, Bob struck it first time. Goal! "Fantasy FC stadium here we come."

Luis Tregenna (10)
Crofton Junior School, Petts Wood

Killing The President

I raced to the cell, the prisoner had escaped. I went to the secret base to investigate what he wanted to do. He wanted to kill the president! Karl spat his tea out as he shouted, "Who would do such a thing?"
The next day, the prisoner went to kill the president. I tried to intercept him and fight him off, he was about to reach his destiny. The president shouted, "Help! Anyone, please!" as I sprang into action to kill the mystery man. *Bang!* I shot him. "Thank you," the president said as he came over.

Joshua Tavonga Rusike (11)
Crofton Junior School, Petts Wood

The Mystery Selsi Gand

It all starts here in an enchanted forest and in this forest, not like other forests, is an enchanted house. But anyway let's get on with the main point because we do not have forever. So in this house something mysterious happened and Selsi was on this mission. Selsi's enemy was very powerful and on Selsi's last mission she found out all of the enemy's plans and there were 100! Selsi dressed in her spy Selania's outfit and hid under a table. Soon her enemy came and Selsi saved some of her friends and then partied happily.

Hana McAvoy (8)
Crofton Junior School, Petts Wood

The Ginormous Spider

One lovely, sunny day, someone was walking through the deserted rainforest. She saw a large tree and decided to climb it. When the girl got to the top, she realised there was a dead body lurking on top of a branch. She wondered why it was there and suddenly saw a gigantic spider racing towards her... Running as fast as a cheetah, she rushed away from the spider, almost tripping up on a tree root. She finally found herself out of the terrible rainforest. Feeling relieved, the girl ran back home and all of a sudden, she collapsed and fainted.

Holly Sudduth (9)
Crofton Junior School, Petts Wood

Saving The Orphans!

I was a furious orphan at the ancient Otto's Orphanage. My friends and I kept getting caned by the cunning, mean Mrs Marocco. I had to transform her into a horse to save us. I sprinted to my ragged dormitory. I turned the lamp off and fell asleep.
When I woke up I grabbed my transformation potion, charged to the canteen and ate my disgusting porridge. Then I ran to Mrs Marocco's office and barged in. I threw the blue bubbling potion at her. She howled in surprise as she turned into a gentle, white horse. We all shouted hooray!

Thomas Marshall (8)
Crofton Junior School, Petts Wood

Eva And The Magic Forest

Once upon a time, there was a girl named Eva. Eva's pet owl was sick so she set off to the magic forest. So off she set. When she got there, she went in and, all of a sudden, she was lost! Eva walked a little and found a bird that talked to her. Eva was amazed.
The bird said, "I know where the berries that you are looking for are."
Eva replied, "Where?"
"First," said the bird, "you must help me get home, it's by the berry bush." So Eva helped the bird and the bird helped Eva.

Sophie Copeland (8)
Crofton Junior School, Petts Wood

The Story Of A Key

Once upon a time, there lived a dog named Dog! He had been locked up inside the house and the only way out was to find a key. He looked outside, seeing birds and cats. "Why can't I get out?" Dog complained. Then, out of the corner of Dog's eye, he saw a key on the high shelf.
Then a cat came strolling in, he climbed to the high shelf. "Can you get that key?" Dog said. The cat knocked it down. "Thanks."
"What are you doing?" said the owner. "Come on, Ralph. Come on, Dog."

Andreas Theodorou (8)
Crofton Junior School, Petts Wood

The Quest

One day, but not just a normal day, a girl called Sapphira was at home the night before Christmas. Suddenly, she got a notification. *Who could that be?* she thought. Again she thought, *who is it?* Then she realised it was a quest. She ran to her school to meet the Master. She met with the Master, he told her to catch a thief. Sapphira did as she was told. She ran everywhere, no thief. 'Til she saw movement, she ran towards it, *bang!* Sapphira found the thief. It was a miracle. She took the thief to the Master.

Isla Shenol (9)
Crofton Junior School, Petts Wood

Tomb Hunt

Lara jumped out of the helicopter as it blew up, the fire went off. Lara glanced around for shelter, she ran there and slipped, rolled then got up. Her vision was blurry, she couldn't see anything. A shine blinded her. She saw a man. He had an axe-like hook. He started to charge but Lara was still on the floor, covered in blood and mud. She got up and ran. She saw a village. The tall shadow-like man jumped off a roof with blazing eyes. Suddenly, *slam!* Blood spilling everywhere, her eyes shut. The man held an artefact up...

Zachary Scanlon (11)

Crofton Junior School, Petts Wood

Lortal Whitagher

One day, a boy woke up and his dad had disappeared. For a while, he didn't mind. That day, a villain, Box-Man, came. Tomorrow, Lortal would set off on a wild quest to get the sacred box cutters to kill Box-Man. Then he heard a noise, it was coming from the box that his mum said never to open. However, he didn't care. Then, on the news, he heard someone say Box-Man was coming to Lortal's house. He found the box cutters. The fight started, but it only went on for ten seconds. Obviously, Lortal Whitagher won the intense fight.

Lorcan Gallagher (9)
Crofton Junior School, Petts Wood

A Family Mystery

I had until sunset to find the only key to the vault of my family history with my sister, Midnight. We were on a beach trying to find it before Eric, our cousin.
In the morning, we travelled in our machine to Mars. There, we glimpsed the chest, before spotting Eric. We plunged towards him and fell into a cave. Vines covered the wall, just big enough to climb. There was a glint in one of them. The key! Once I'd caught it I scrambled up, Midnight behind me, and we opened the chest together. Our family history was inside!

Isabella Moriarty (10)
Crofton Junior School, Petts Wood

Next Gen Society

The rocket took off, she took a breath. Percy held her hand and closed his eyes. Hastily, the rocket faltered, they had landed on an unknown planet. It was full of wildlife and greenery. Percy stepped out, plants all turned to him. In the distance, a dome full of robots were using plants to make new bots, so they could help with climate change. Mackenzie decided to call it Next Generation Environment Centre as they were trying to help us. They got back in the rocket and flew back home. From then they were known as the Next-Gen Duo.

Jessica Viney (11)
Crofton Junior School, Petts Wood

The Desert Trap

"I have ten days," said Jon Hardstone, an ex-convict turned MI5 agent. Jon had been trapped by his rival agent Neil Amavi. It turned out that Neil was an undercover rat giving secrets to an organisation trying to destroy the world. Neil had trapped Jon, who was MI5's best agent, in the desert miles away from people. Luckily Jon had some water. He knew that he had to travel twenty-three miles to the secret helipad for desert missions. So he set off on his ruthless trek across the unforgiving climate. Did he succeed...?

Mason Bartley (10)
Crofton Junior School, Petts Wood

The Murder

I raced to the cell wondering what Uncle Jim would say. Did they drown? Did they die from an illness? What happened to Mum and Dad? As I got to the cell I could see through the crooked bars old scrawny Jim. I asked, "Jim, what happened to Mum and Dad, did they drown? What happened?"
With a croak like a toad he replied, "Now, now, calm down. They were killed around five years ago now. Somebody killed them."
I then raced to the telephone box. I went spinning. I knew what to do. I had to change the past.

Poppy Adams (10)
Crofton Junior School, Petts Wood

The Missing Treasure

One day, I was walking on an empty, isolated island to find treasure that no one had found before. I'd been travelling for days on the huge island because my map said that the treasure was somewhere over there. I really wanted to be the first one to find it and keep the treasure. I hoped I was somewhere near the treasure, as I wanted to find it before night. Suddenly, I saw something shiny. I felt really excited and dug on that spot. I found something incredible - it was a golden, glistening, and really sparkly treasure chest!

Myra Bachwani (9)
Crofton Junior School, Petts Wood

The Curse

What's that scroll on my bedroom floor?... It read, 'Dear Tilly, you have been chosen to find a ring then shine it to the sun, then it will break the curse. After several years of continuous daylight, the sky will turn dark and the stars will come out. You have until sunrise'. Ten minutes later Tilly burst out of the house. She saw something glowing under a tree. It was the ring, she picked it up and shone it to the sun. There was an explosion in the sky and the curse had been broken and Tilly had done it!

Caitlin Logue (9)

Crofton Junior School, Petts Wood

Christmas Kidnap

Once upon a time, there lived a nice family. It was near Christmas, five days away to be precise, and my mum went to my school for parents' evening. You know, I bet you've had one, but let's get to the point, okay? That night, the Minotaur kidnapped my parents and he had them tied to a chair in his classroom. I was thinking about blowing the school up with gunpowder but that would've been copying Guy Fawkes. So I thought I would go over there. When I did, the Minotaur welcomed me in. It turned out it was nice.

Gus Bartlett (9)
Crofton Junior School, Petts Wood

The Locked Room

Oakley was a ten-year-old girl who was told not to go in the dark, locked room. But one day she decided to go in. There wasn't much in there, until she pulled a lever, and the floor sank into a room filled with machines. She looked at them. They were ancient Tudor punishment machines. Oakley sat in one of the torture machines. Oakley suddenly screamed and cried for help, but no one heard her. A few hours went by, and her mother didn't even notice. The next day, Oakley was nowhere to be seen. Never, ever, ever again!

Suraiya Beckford (10)
Crofton Junior School, Petts Wood

Valhalla

There was a man called Odin and he wanted to get to Valhalla. But he kept killing people. So he decided he would find powerful-looking warriors to kill him. So he set off on a long journey. Soon, he found a powerful warrior. So he thought, *they will kill me*. But soon he killed the warrior. "Oh no!" he cried. After killing ten more powerful men, he started to worry a lot. Soon there were ten warriors and they were powerful. So Odin got killed and ended up in Valhalla and fought and ate over and over again.

Purvi Upreti (8)
Crofton Junior School, Petts Wood

A Disaster In Pompeii

Deep within the mountain, a disaster was brewing. I had until midday to stop a devastating eruption of Mt. Vesuvius. The year was 79AD and it was all up to me to save Pompeii. I set off into the collapsing passageways of Mt. Vesuvius and had to remove a giant boulder from blocking my way to the magma chamber. Then, all of a sudden, I broke through into the boiling magma pit. Immediately I started to tunnel a channel away from Pompeii, to direct the lava flow away. I sprinted away from the volcano. *Boom!* It worked!

Ryan Horsfield (10)
Crofton Junior School, Petts Wood

The Curse

A helicopter hovered above a jungle holding Midas and his brother Brutas. Midas was a super god and Brutas was a god but the helicopter got shot down by the guards of the curse. The helicopter went spinning and they jumped out and it hit the ground and blew up. Midas and Brutas walked. Suddenly they got ambushed by the guards and they shot and killed Brutas. Midas killed them and found the temple. A lava boss merged and Midas ran and turned him into gold. He found the curse. Using his gun he shot it, destroying the curse.

Nico Currell (11)

Crofton Junior School, Petts Wood

Storm At Sea

In the middle of the sea, a massive storm approached. The ship was tossed about like a toy. Not knowing what to do, Okcor threw a chain into the air. He was instantly struck by lightning, it sparkled brightly, lighting up the ship. Suddenly, a bolt of lightning struck the side of the ship. Slowly, the boat fell on its side. Okcor gasped for a breath of air, but then his helmet got struck by lightning, electrocuting Okcor, making the ocean light up with thunder. Paralysed, Okcor fell down, down, down, into the ocean below.

Alex Jessop (9)
Crofton Junior School, Petts Wood

The Unexpected Adventure

Plodding through the forest, I was enjoying the blazing sun and twittering birds. Just when I decided to go home, a growling noise broke the silence. What was that? I swivelled around. Out of the gloom, a beast emerged. It was a human being and a bull merged together, mishapenly. I just had time to dive before the beast pounced. As its horns stuck to a tree, I pulled one out. Then I was ready. When the monster charged, I thrust the horn in front of me and the monster disintegrated. As I scanned the forest, it seemed dead.

Darren Chun-Hei Chan (10)
Crofton Junior School, Petts Wood

The Beast

Aiden is shy but loves adventure. He saw a monster. He started running to it. The leader was not pleased. Aiden met a lot of creatures. First, an alpha wolf. The beast was not a problem and in seven seconds it was dead. He entered an overgrown jungle, fought a few giant bees, then set up camp, ate some boar and slept but then...the monster came. He picked up a dagger and cut his vines. It screeched suddenly. The leader appeared and killed it. They went home and had a feast. Turns out the monster was the most evil ever.

Jake Clarke (9)
Crofton Junior School, Petts Wood

Adventurers

I heard a roar. It was very loud. Me and my friend, Brooke, were really scared. We shoved the bushes away and saw a furious lion. It looked really angry. As we hid quickly, we heard steps. We were panicking but then we heard a squeak. And then stomps. I whispered to Brooke, "I'm going to peek." So I peeked and then gasped. I saw a little mouse. I carefully sat down again. I sighed in relief. It was just a mouse. We walked carefully through the bushes and then we opened a bush carefully. Guess what we saw?

Isla Kidd (8)

Crofton Junior School, Petts Wood

Captain Bubbles

Deep in the jungle, I was running from the deadliest villain, called Hockmor. I ran to hide as Hockmor followed. I jumped out and was fighting with my trusty sword. I stumbled to the ground, I had to run to my hideout. There, in another world, was the hideout. In the hideout, there were magical creatures. I, Captain Bubbles, got all of them and went out to defeat Hockmor. We battled, we were winning. I got Shell, my turtle, he squirted ice and Hockmor froze. I stabbed my knife and Hockmor died, never to be seen again.

Izzy Prestage (9)
Crofton Junior School, Petts Wood

The Dark Planet

Suddenly, I woke up in a gloomy, mystical world and surprisingly, not my bedroom! As I wandered around on this new, eye-catching planet, I saw a dark, minuscule figure. My bed was a rock. As I dashed to the figure, I could see a sparkly, crystal-clear gem in the distance. As I strolled up to the scary figure, it stared directly into my eyes. I felt shivers rushing down my spine! I took a loud gulp, as loud as a tiger's roar! I had reached the gem. Then I felt a hand. Suddenly, my heart stopped beating instantly...

James Doye (9)

Crofton Junior School, Petts Wood

The Storm King

We were sitting in class waiting for the bell when a huge bang came from the gate. Eagerly, hundreds of little heads peered through the windows to see a tall, 100-foot person made out of the wind. Making his way over with smaller versions of him, one by one children were sliced into pieces by the horns of the king. Me and my friend Sid got on the roof. Cornered. Suddenly a shining sword appeared, I grabbed it. I jumped up and sliced his face. Screams from behind me signalled that Sid was dead but so was the monster.

Frank Wyatt (10)
Crofton Junior School, Petts Wood

The Strange Disappearance

At sunset, a baby unicorn was stolen by an evil witch ghoul. She wanted to cut off the unicorn, Sparkle's, golden horn so she could make a magic potion to keep herself young. Later that evening, a little princess called Mia, had a pet but it was Sparkle. When she went missing it broke Mia's heart. On a late afternoon, Mia heard a call - it was her pet unicorn. Quickly she flew into a cave and found the unicorn strapped to a rock. Mia unstrapped the unicorn. On the way back to the castle, they flew joyfully.

Isabel Taylor (9)

Crofton Junior School, Petts Wood

Candy Land

Once upon a time, a boy named Bode woke up but he wasn't in his bedroom. He was in this place that looked a little like Candy Land because rainbow-coloured sprinkles were raining down on him, and candy canes too! There were also jelly beans leading a path. Bode started to enjoy it, until a massive candy cane rained down, hitting him and knocking him out. Then suddenly, Bode found himself lying on the mucky, hard kitchen floor. He stood up and realised it was just a dream but he'd been sleepwalking as well.

Jessica Kelly (9)
Crofton Junior School, Petts Wood

Keys

A long time ago a powerful locksmith created a key that changes to what your mind wants. Now this key has fallen into the wrong hands, a person who wants to take over the world. Jack. And now there's me, running tirelessly, chasing him. Jumping between narrow cracks in the earth waiting for him to make one wrong move. It was at one jump he fell. The key, it seemed was calling out to me. I came upon a graveyard, the one where the locksmith lay. There was a photo of him and then I realised he was my ancestor...

Ruby Clarke (11)
Crofton Junior School, Petts Wood

The Gem

As the gem twinkled in the light, Myles crept up towards the stand. His hazel eyes glued onto the stone, he told his friends to stay back. His hand reached forward, ready to grab the gem, when a shout from his friends grew louder. His hand grasped onto the stone and a blast of energy went throughout the cave. A grin was on his face but got wiped off as soon as the stone exploded. Myles reached out his hand and Scarlett grabbed it. The power spread throughout their bodies and they were safe. Or so they thought...

Georgia Peel (11)

Crofton Junior School, Petts Wood

Shape-Shifting Reality

It was 23:08 and Nora had just got back from her 24-hour shift. She was exhausted. As she changed into her pyjamas, Nora heard noises from her floorboards. She hesitated to look. A few minutes later, Nora decided to look. She ran to the shed to get a crowbar. As she got back into the room the door was shaking, she yanked it. Some wind pulled her in. As she got pulled, she came through the other side. It was the same? Then the portal evaporated. Someone came in, Nora woke up. It was just a dream... or was it?

Grace Angier (10)

Crofton Junior School, Petts Wood

Life Backfired

I was alone. Well, never mind; I needed to find the evil Queen Mary and kill her. You see, she almost killed my twin Maria. That was my quest! I set off. I heard the sound of footsteps. What should I do? I hid behind a tree. My ninja skills actually paid off! That moment, Maria, my twin came walking past. Phew! I asked her, "Where we should go? That way?"
We walked until we got to the end of a cliff. These were my last moments; she pushed me off. How dare she! She was working for Queen Mary!

Rakshaya Rajesh (11)
Crofton Junior School, Petts Wood

Gloomy Mystery

As I entered the gloomy jungle I felt petrified, there were cobwebs and bushes. I walked around trying to find somewhere to sleep, all there was squelchy mud and leaves. I tried my best to make something with it. I made a small hammock to stay in until it started to rain heavily. I was soaked so I made a small den with big bamboo, heavy kits of bark and sticks, but oh no, now I was sleeping on mud! Then a lion caught me, my den was ruined, my whole adventure was ruined. Let's just say I'm gone now!

Sidney Mae Lewis (10)
Crofton Junior School, Petts Wood

The Fairy Friends

Once upon a time, there lived a girl named Stella. One day, Stella and her mother went for a picnic in the forest. When they reached the forest, they sat on a bench and set the picnic up. As Stella was waiting she took a stroll down the forest. As she did that she saw something sitting on a rock. It was a fairy! They talked together though they didn't know each other well. They became friends but as that happened, it was time for Stella to go. The fairy made a friendship bracelet and gave it to Stella.

Amy Anooj (9)

Crofton Junior School, Petts Wood

The Hideaway Gang

My heart was pounding. My eyes darted around, looking for places to hide, but there was nowhere. I could hear their voices behind me. I had to find my mum. I jumped down into the ditch, hoping they wouldn't check it out. Thankfully, they ran past. I jumped out and sprinted back to their hideout, hoping to find her. Then I heard shouts and a gunshot. A bullet whizzed past my head. I was so close. I could hear her calling me. Then something hit the back of my head. All I felt was pain. All I saw was red.

Dexter Roberts (9)
Crofton Junior School, Petts Wood

Adventure Hunters

I woke up in a deep, dark cave. Small beams of light peeking through. I walked out with strong light roaring at me. I started to walk until I found an off-road car. I hopped in and without a second lions and hyenas were behind me. I drove through forests, sharp corners, shallow rivers until I lost them. I found a boat. Then I saw shades of green. Crocodiles. I hopped in the boat and drove until I came to a large waterfall. I turned around driving through the crocodiles and then I hopped out. I was safe!

James Foster (10)
Crofton Junior School, Petts Wood

The Potion

Harland ran for the bike and rode into the golden sunlight. He had just come from a secret base which was hidden perfectly in Egypt. He was an athletic, smart guy working for Her Majesty's Secret Service. He was trying to stop a madman from drinking a dangerous potion, making him immortal. He drove and drove but the man was always one step ahead of him. So he decided to stop him at all costs. He knew how he would do it. The fighter jet was ready to be crashed into the man, so he hit the accelerator.

Sam Doyle (10)

Crofton Junior School, Petts Wood

Lost In Space

When Jeff and Bob were playing one day, they made a pretend rocket that had a pretend engine with a real button that would do nothing if they clicked it. Later on, they decided to click it and surprisingly, it set off to space with Bob in it. They were lucky to have real helmets on. Bob was screaming for help, so Jeff made another one and it worked. He was off too. Bob was miles away from Jeff, but Jeff's rocket was faster. He searched for Bob for ages, then found him. Then made it back down safely.

Aidan Barnes (10)
Crofton Junior School, Petts Wood

Sophie And The Ocean!

The alarm went. Time to get up to go on holiday. Sophie got up and walked out of bed. Her mum and dad and Liam (her four-year-old brother) drove to the airport.
Finally, after two hours, they arrived in Spain. She jumped straight into the refreshing pool. As soon as she did this, she saw an amazing thing. She saw a whale, a seahorse, a stingray and a starfish. The whale was injured but she kindly helped it. Then she heard a shout, it was her mum. She had to go. Will she ever see the animals again?

Belle (10)
Crofton Junior School, Petts Wood

The Mystery Story

Me and Bailey went to a haunted house and in the creepy house there was a door that wouldn't open. Me and Bailey used all our strength. Suddenly, the door creaked open, me and Bailey were terrified. We were brave and went inside. In a blink of an eye, we heard water... It was a rotten pool. We went closer until... We fell in! We discovered that there was a glowing key. We took the key and walked. Meanwhile, we saw a shadow of a door, we went over and opened it... We gasped, it was a treasure box...

Emily Denton (10)
Crofton Junior School, Petts Wood

The Adventurer

Once upon a time, Ragnar the Mighty set off on a quest to find a worthy opponent. "I will find an enemy to kill me and go to the mighty Valhalla," yelled Ragnar the Mighty. He set off on a quest to go to Valhalla. He found a beast that he thought was a worthy opponent. Ragnar charged at the mighty beast. The beast rapidly ran at Ragnar and they had a mighty battle. In the end, Ragnar the Mighty slew the beast with his majestic sword and stabbed it. Ragnar the Mighty went back to his house.

William Jansze (8)

Crofton Junior School, Petts Wood

Secret Door

Once upon a time, there was a girl called Daisy. She was at home playing with her amazing brother and sister. They were all playing hide-and-seek but then Daisy felt cold and said, "I am cold, so I am going to go upstairs to put a jumper on." She went upstairs and put on a fantastic, amazing, and pretty jumper. She looked at herself in the mirror and she saw a glowing thing behind the mirror. There was a secret door and she saw beautiful jewels. She closed the door and went to play again.

Betsy Bannister (8)
Crofton Junior School, Petts Wood

The Item And The Dragon

Once, a little girl in Moscow saw black snow on Christmas Eve and saw something in the sky. It was a dragon, how strange. The little girl's name was Sen Morshe. She went out of bed to the train station in the dead of night. The train she saw was called the Dragon. Sen Morshe went on it and went to another station. Then she saw the dragon. She followed the dragon and had a magic item that defeated the horrible, loathsome dragon. She went back on the train, back to her home, and went back to bed.

Samuel Slater (8)
Crofton Junior School, Petts Wood

Adventure Hunters

I was at the bottom of an ancient large volcano that could erupt any second. My aim was to get a sample of boiling hot lava. This task was very dangerous and I had to be ready for anything bad that could happen. Shockingly this volcano was so big that I'd been walking for fifteen minutes and I was a quarter of the way up. Luckily I could see a little crack of lava. Suddenly I could hear a deafening roar echo around me. It was about to erupt, I got my stuff and ran with fear down the volcano.

George Bridle (11)
Crofton Junior School, Petts Wood

The Story Of The Plane Crash

On a normal, misty morning a family was on a plane. They were going on holiday when, all of a sudden, their plane hit turbulence. Because of that, they crashed in the middle of the ocean. No one had heard from the family since that day. Then, one day, an explorer visited the deserted island to see if the story of the plane crash was true. She had explored through the island, which was next to the deep ocean, and there was the family. They looked like they weren't going to be able to survive.

Kayla Thornton (11)
Crofton Junior School, Petts Wood

Ravin And The Crow

It starts with a young girl, Ravin. Ravin was on a quest to Bird Land! Suddenly, an electric crow bit her! She realised she had to get to Bird Land. She set off early in the morning, then walked and walked and walked. Finally, she reached Bird Land but there was a huge sea, too wide to cross, and she only had 'til sunset, which was two hours away. Surprisingly, a beautiful bird came down. Ravin was so amazed! The bird lifted her into the sky then she arrived at Bird Land. She was so excited!

Anya Whiting (8)
Crofton Junior School, Petts Wood

Jungle

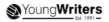

The magic key glowed and took them to the jungle. As they landed, the magic key disappeared, they couldn't find it anywhere. Tommy looked under the leaves but it was not there. Tommy asked the monkey to help him look for the magic key in the jungle. The monkey found the key on the ground. The key on the ground was covered in leaves. So Tommy said thank you to the monkey for finding the key on the ground. Then he walked away so he went back home with his magic key and he was very happy.

Matthew Taiwo (10)
Crofton Junior School, Petts Wood

The Mystery

As I opened my eyes I saw a dozen bees swarming around me. Shocked at that moment in time I got up and rolled away. I was very scared so I jumped in the pool and they flew away. I got out of the pool and all of a sudden I saw a door that looked suspicious. So I went over to it and there was a key that said,
'unlock the door'. So I did and it glowed in the lock and opened up without me touching it and you'll never guess what I saw in the doorway...

Caitlin Shelley (10)
Crofton Junior School, Petts Wood

The Conman

I had until noon to find the cave. I was going to give up but a clue was on my door, 'under the water'. I got my swimsuit on and got ready. I found it at last! I went to the dark cave, I had a flashlight luckily and then there it was, the box of treasure. I swam back to the surface and ran to the man who told me to find the box, his name was Noah. He had tricked me. He wanted money and gave me nothing. I wanted to kill him! I will get him!

Eviee Howelles (10)
Crofton Junior School, Petts Wood

Little Otto

The first day that it happened, my tree grew. Every time it grew, something appeared next to it or in the small box. On the final day, the tree was so tall that it broke the void and I could see a bigger void above. So that's when I got the idea that I was now able to escape the void so I did. I had escaped to learn that I was on some sort of gigantic object. I spotted a wall, it smiled at me and told me my name was Otto and I had been dead.

Tia Veneta (10)

Crofton Junior School, Petts Wood

Valhalla

Once upon a time, there was a man called Leo. He was adventurous and never scared. He was trying to find a magic door. The door was hidden in a lair guarded by an evil giant. Behind the door was a map to his true love's castle. He finally killed the giant and, exhausted, entered the lair and found the magic door. The door opened into a dark forest. He shook a tree and from it dropped a map. It glowed. He'd found it!

Leo Coello (9)

Crofton Junior School, Petts Wood

The Truth Of Geography

We'd have to go to 10BCE to find the first map projection. Most people were attacking us. We found the creator and demanded, "Give us the truth of geography."
He said, "Go to the next projection."
We had to go through time to the Mercator projection. We somehow spawned in Antarctica, so we teleported to where he was. I and Suhail said, "We need the truth of geography."
The CEO said, "Go to Robinson time."
We got so mad, we punched him and teleported to Robinson time. We immediately told him our quest. He said, "The truth is all unrevealed."

Suhaib Diriya (9)
Edward Wilson Primary School, Westminster

William's Mission

William was a determined young boy who wanted to save our Earth from dying. One day, he started collecting rubbish from everywhere. The people in William's town were frustrated because of William's idea. That night, a man dumped a huge amount of garbage in front of his house. As soon as William found out, he contacted his landlord and filed a complaint about him. William was furious but remained calm. Fortunately, the man who threw the garbage was fined almost £10,000! William continued to collect all the rubbish in his area. Eventually, he was rewarded £100,000 from the honourable Queen!

Yousif Qazizada (10)
Edward Wilson Primary School, Westminster

Heroic Herioelle Of Mars

As she got hit by lightning, she lay motionless. Tears streaming down Herioelle's face. She was in hospital and couldn't move her limbs. Then she realised she wasn't in a hospital, she was in a gloomy forest... on Mars! After all the trauma, she saw a cute little alien. His name was Simoytotu. He screamed, "Herioelle! Come quick! We need you to defeat the one and only Sinoctodiles! If you do, you will go back to Earth."
She scampered outside and used lightning powers, from her incident. Heroically, after seconds of fighting Sinoctodiles Herioelle was known as Herioellekihero!

Roqayah Al-Memar (11)
Edward Wilson Primary School, Westminster

The Golden Mystery Eye

Once, there were two boys called John and Max who had parents who'd passed away. It was Christmas! It was snowy! It was beautiful! As I was in my house, looking at the freezing snow, the doorbell rang, it was Max. Once I opened the door for Max, I noticed that there was a very loud bomb that'd exploded.

"I want my gold!" said a man.

"Who was that?" said Max.

"The Emperor!" said John.

"He wants the golden eye," said Max. "Quick, hide it."

Once the Emperor came to us, the two boys gasped.

"Where is it?" he said.

Layth Merza (10)

Edward Wilson Primary School, Westminster

Monster In The House

In the house, there was a boy called Fred. His parents were at work. He would go to the closet every day so he could see a monster. It never popped up but when there was no hope, Fred's eyes gazed on who he'd found.

He said, "Hello, my name is Jeffrey."

Fred said, "Awesome."

Then Jeffrey said, "Don't tell anyone."

Fred said, "Okay." They both watched TV. They found out that Fred's mum was captured. They searched the city at midnight so no one would see Jeffrey. They found Fred's mum and dad and lived forever together.

Hussain Al-Ansari (9)

Edward Wilson Primary School, Westminster

An Adventure

Once upon a time, there was a wild explorer. She would always go on adventurers and find ancient treasures. "Hi," she said. "As you can see, I'm on an adventure," she said while trying to open a door. Not just an ordinary door - a door leading to Tutankhamun's tomb!
"Just imagine how many priceless artefacts there are inside that tomb," she said.
After some time, she got the door to open.
"Oh, and by the way, my name is Lana," Lana said.
Once she got into the tomb, she decided to just glance at the artefacts. The door shut!

Diyala Ahmed (9)
Edward Wilson Primary School, Westminster

The Daring Robbery Of The Dragon's Jewels

Anthony didn't know how to rob the dragon's jewels. It hadn't happened for one hundred years up until now. The dragon was mightily fierce. He would spit scorching fire that could burn metal ten times stronger than steel. Anthony trembled. What was he going to do? Suddenly, Anthony walked along the gloomy castle hallway when the beast of a dragon suddenly awoke from his slumber. It flapped its razor-sharp wings and started breathing balls of fire out of its mouth. Anthony knew this was the end. He just remembered he had a sword! He slew the dragon. The jewels appeared...

Aiden To (10)
Edward Wilson Primary School, Westminster

The Beautiful Little Mermaid

Once upon a time, there lived a little mermaid whose name was Diamond. After a few days, she went to an abandoned place. Suddenly, Diamond found a tunnel. She was curious about what was inside. She went inside the tunnel and found a boy named Mohamed. Mohamed and Diamond were talking about life and Mohamed said that he was lost in that awful place. Diamond said that there was a tunnel leading back outside. Mohamed told Diamond that his parents were gone. Diamond wanted to solve his parents' mystery. After Diamond solved the mystery, Mohamed and his parents lived happily.

Maram Jaf (8)
Edward Wilson Primary School, Westminster

The Orb

There once were three people called Jack, Jerry and Kim. Their mum said, "Let's go on a camping trip."

So they said, "Yes!" So they packed their stuff. When they got there, they went to explore around the forest. Suddenly, a ball in a cage was shining in their eyes. They were worried, so they backed away.

But a figure came and said, "Hello, my small dears."

They could tell he wanted the orb and they wanted it as well, so they battled. The mum, Jack, Jerry, and Kim punched him and got the orb. They all said, "Yay!"

Omar Sharar (8)

Edward Wilson Primary School, Westminster

A Magical World

It was a beautiful day. Tom went for a walk in the park. He was enjoying his time there when suddenly, he came across a bridge. Tom saw a bright light which he went through. It took him to a new world. A beautiful location with butterflies and unicorns and a magical view of the forest and dolphins in the blue, shiny river.

Suddenly, a voice called, "You okay, Sir?"

Tom was anxious and furious to find out that he was rushed to hospital after a very unpleasant accident, of falling into the river. He was, thankfully, alive.

Ayoub Murad (7)
Edward Wilson Primary School, Westminster

Monster Hunter

Once upon a time, there was a boy called Saruto Uhumaki who left school at the age of twelve to become a hunter. I know what you're thinking, what is a hunter? A hunter is a person who slays monsters, and Saruto wanted to become a hunter to get revenge for his brother. The monsters killed his brother. A few weeks later, he found gold and diamonds. Four years later, Saruto found a cave and saw a man. It was half-human, half-monster. That monster was Saruto's brother! He was shocked but then they started fighting and the monsters vanished.

Shazaad Alizada (10)
Edward Wilson Primary School, Westminster

The Lost Girl

Once, there was a girl called Amanda who had an enchanted life. One day, she went into the forest to discover something but it started to get darker and rainy. When she got to the middle of the forest, there were two pathways but she didn't know which one to go through. When she finally went through one, there were weird noises and she got scared. "Help!" she repeatedly yelled, but no one heard her. Then she had an idea. "What if I make a fire and someone sees the smoke?" Thankfully, Amanda got helped by a stranger.

Mais El-Zarif (11)
Edward Wilson Primary School, Westminster

The Drawings That Came To Life

Once upon a time, there was a girl named Uzma and she loved to draw but once, her drawing became real. She was shocked so she ran downstairs and told her parents but they didn't believe her, although she was telling the truth. She thought, *why don't I save the Earth?* Then she quickly put on her shoes, grabbed paper, and ran outside and started drawing a bin, signs, and lots of other things. She was out for too long and she didn't know. One hour later, she realised and ran home. Her parents cried, "Honey!"

Uzma Qazizada (8)
Edward Wilson Primary School, Westminster

Lilly's Adventure

It was Lilly's birthday. Her mum pushed a big present into her room. She opened it, it was a unicorn! The creature had a white body and a pink mane. She jumped on without thinking and the unicorn took her away. First, they went to Candyland, then to Toyland where teddies and dolls waved at her. Finally they went to Wishland, where your wishes come true! Lilly wished for a dollhouse and she got one.
"Lilly, wake up!"
Lilly woke with a start. It was a dream... or was it? There was magic unicorn dust on the floor!

Dora Tan (9)
Edward Wilson Primary School, Westminster

The Superpower

Once upon a time, there was a boy called Max. He loved sailing. One day, he went looking for a treasure. He got lost. He found an island, so he stopped. He found a treasure chest. Inside there was an apple. He ate the apple. When he tried to make fire, fire blasted out. He was shocked. He found out that he could make anything he wanted. Unfortunately, he couldn't control it. Then he heard a voice saying, "Relax." So he did. Amazingly, it worked. He made a boat and went home. At home, he helped everyone that needed help.

Ibrahim Arbab (10)
Edward Wilson Primary School, Westminster

Saving Someone

There was a girl called Isabelle and she was having a nice day until she saw something in her bedroom. It was a devil. One day, she was tidying her bedroom. She went to the kitchen and after two minutes, her room was messy. Her mum saw her room and she was disappointed. The girl was so confused, what'd happened to her room? When she was walking outside, she found a boy. She really liked him. The boy wanted to save the day and called a monster saver. So the monster saver sucked the monster into the gross, smelly drain.

Zaynab Jannah (8)

Edward Wilson Primary School, Westminster

Royal Relations

It was a nice, sunny day so I decided to ride my skateboard in the garden. As I was doing the super cool twirly trick, my skateboard hit a colossal lump in the grass! *Huh? Since when was there a huge mound in the grass?* Out of curiosity, I started to dig! I found a note mysteriously folded up inside a bottle. I quickly unfolded the note - it was a family tree! The queen and king, then my grandparents! My mum and dad, and me, Natalie, then my brother Nathan! Was this really the truth? Am I actually a princess?

Aleena Ali (10)
Edward Wilson Primary School, Westminster

Good Change

This is a story about Jack and his mother, getting transformed upside down. Jack and his mother prepared to move to a new location. Sadly, he was a distance from his friends which made him very furious and petrified about the new city he would live in. Jack worried if he was going to like his new school. But he was very anxious and excited to live with his mother and grandparents. In the end, it was fantastic, an extraordinary change. And he went to a club and he liked to play football and tennis and basketball.

Anmar Murad (10)
Edward Wilson Primary School, Westminster

The World Of Dreams

Once upon a time, Princess Nounou lived happily in a palace with her family and her cat. Under her bed, there was a box with a magic key that opened the cave that took them to the World of Dreams. The evil Nana heard the key, so she disguised herself as a kind grandmother to enter her room, looking for the key and escaping with it. She started looking for the cave guard who did not let anyone approach except Princess Nounou. He told her that she couldn't enter because the key only worked with the Princess.

Noussaiba Boudi (7)

Edward Wilson Primary School, Westminster

The Lost City Of Jewels

There once was a girl named Alexa. She had two siblings, one twin sister and one brother. She was home alone one day with her pet kitten. She was in her bed when she heard crashing. She dashed to the living room only to see a missing gold watch and a very valuable vase. The next day she went out to a deserted forest with her siblings. She decided to search the forest for the criminal. Later on, gold coins and necklaces were found. She found someone sleeping with a bag. She arrested him and returned the items.

Khadja Mohamed (9)

Edward Wilson Primary School, Westminster

Catching A Horrible And Mean Baddy

Once upon a time, there was me, my crewmates, and a horrible, mean baddy. One night, we went home to sleep. Suddenly, the alarm rang and we knew that it was the baddy. So after that, we went to the security camera and he was stealing things from people. So we went outside, we put slippery shampoo out and then the baddy ran and he slipped. So after we called the police and they came, so then the police picked him up and then he went to prison. After, we went to our homes and went into our comfortable beds.

Janna Merza (7)
Edward Wilson Primary School, Westminster

Meteorite Mayhem

One day, I decided to look through a telescope at night to look at the sky. When I did, I discovered a large rock heading towards Earth. I felt like I needed to do the right thing and take care of the situation. I had recently gained new powers and decided it was time to use them. The meteorite was also boiling, which made it more difficult. I went to the meteorite and slinged it away from Earth with my super strength. I then came back down to Earth and I was glad that everything was still in place.

Mysha Begum (10)
Edward Wilson Primary School, Westminster

The Magic Arose

Wandering through the dark forest, out of nowhere, my hands started shaking. All of a sudden, I rose into the air. My heart started to pound really fast, I thought I was having a heart attack! Then a lady stepped out of a deserted well. I felt petrified, you don't know how petrified I was. She started speaking gibberish and weirdly I could understand it - I mean, I really could understand it, amazing right? It took me a while to figure this out but I think it's one of my own superpowers.

Zubaydah Aktar (11)
Edward Wilson Primary School, Westminster

The Creature

Once upon a time, there was a park with a camp surrounded by a big, foggy cloud. No one lived in the camp, it was abandoned. But only one person lived there, or should I say, a creature. No one knew about it, only one boy. He was six years old. He told everyone. No one listened. Then, one day, he ran away with a camera for proof. He heard something, it sounded like a lion, it sounded like a wolf. And then it surrounded him. He wasn't fast enough. Then the creature fell into a pond.

Ryan Khaled (9)
Edward Wilson Primary School, Westminster

The Wicked Witch

One day, in the Amazon, a boy went on a dangerous journey to steal a treasure chest full of fortunes. But there was this wicked witch who had the chest and the key. You won't believe where she hid the key! Her mouth! So she had to be in a deep sleep so he could steal the key but she never slept, so he got a poison to make her sleep and she did. He managed to find the key and brought a metal detector and he looked and looked and *bam!* He found the chest and the fortune.

Berna Gashi (10)
Edward Wilson Primary School, Westminster

The Great Tale Of Naruto

So there once was a boy called Naruto. He was close friends with Sasuke but once they got into a fight. They both lost an arm so Naruto got a robotic arm and Sasuke didn't get one. Then Naruto married a girl and he had a kid called Boruto. Naruto and Sasuke were friends. Sasuke taught Boruto many things and he grew up to be the strongest person in any clan. And that is the great tale of Naruto.

Mohammed Al-Mansarawi (10)
Edward Wilson Primary School, Westminster

School Mystery

One gloomy night, me and my friend were roaming around the school at twelve o'clock. We came across a creepy abandoned hall. We walked down scared. All of a sudden my friend heard something. We stopped and listened. We ran away after we heard something but then my friend wanted to go back down.

We managed to get to the bottom of the hall. We saw the door open. Our bodies were trembling. My friend started to cry with fear. We still went in. We saw something that would change our lives. We saw something in a huge box. Treasure!

Raegan Anderson-Agar (9)

Farringdon Academy Inspires, Farringdon

The Magic Key

Once upon a time, I was cleaning my room and my best friend and I were on to my wardrobe. We got all of my clothes and then we found a magical key and at that moment I remembered that I had a door in the back of my wardrobe.
I went downstairs and showed my mum the key.
She said, "Come on then, show me."
I said, "Okay."
We tried the door in the back of my wardrobe. My mum said, "Wow, this room has not changed."
I said, "I will now open the door."
The door clicked.

Rae Brown (8)
Farringdon Academy Inspires, Farringdon

The Monster In School

I always had a suspicion that my teacher was a monster so one day I hid in the stock cupboard. I heard someone say, "Any luck?"
"No," someone said.
What could they be talking about? I looked out and saw a drooling monster. I bit my tongue and held my breath. I had to go then and there.
I ran so fast I forgot about how loud I was. I was baffled about what to do next then I heard a sound so horrifying. I couldn't believe a monster was chasing me. What could I do? Help!

Leo Bell (8)
Farringdon Academy Inspires, Farringdon

The Man In Black

One day I wanted to explore the forest so I did. I saw a strange man but I ignored him. I walked and walked but I saw him again and ran back home. It wasn't there! I screamed with terror!
But then my body tingled. A ball of light lashed out of my hand. I had magic but it could be dangerous so I kept it a secret. What if I was a god? But the man appeared again. Was he the source of my magic? I had to live with the man in the forest which was in jail!

Isaac Dillon (9)
Farringdon Academy Inspires, Farringdon

The Scary School

Once upon a time, me and Jacob were walking to school when we saw Cody. When we got to school there was no one there. It was dark. Me and Cody and Jacob went all over the school, still no one was there, not even a teacher. There was a note saying 'you have till sunrise to find me'.
"Come on, Cody and Jacob. We need to find a monster and slay it."

Tyler Fenbow (8)
Farringdon Academy Inspires, Farringdon

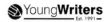

Finding Treasure

I found the secret map and the cross was in the schoolyard so I went and found a shovel. Then I dug and I fell into a cave. I called Cody and Tyler and they came so it was not lonely.
Then I found treasure but it had a lock on. I had a metal detector and it beeped and then I found a key. I unlocked it and I found many coins!

Macie Williams (8)
Farringdon Academy Inspires, Farringdon

The Enchanted Tree

Alissa was running into the dense forest when she clumsily tripped over. As she looked up crystal magic spewed from the heart of a tree standing before her. While Alissa gaped in awe, an icy cold wind seemed to push her fragile body towards the tree, as if it were saying "Don't be afraid." Stumbling towards the tree, she was shoved towards it. Unsurprisingly, she fell through. Squinting, Alissa noticed her surroundings. It seemed like paradise. Gnomes, plants, cottages all gathered around her. Suddenly she glanced behind her. Nothing. Where was the tree? How was she supposed to get home?

Lexi Buck (11)
Lakes Primary School, Redcar

The Iced Death Of Spiral Tower

As I looked up I saw the frost dragon we'd been trying to murder. It roared intensely, shaking the mountain we were on. The person next to me was a ferocious fighter, she'd longed for this moment. She attacked the dragon's head and... missed. The dragon froze her and thankfully the wizard used a fireball and he freed her. Then the dragon bit and mangled the fighter.

The wizard used 'inflict wounds' and sliced parts of the dragon's stomach open, showing its insides. I then pulled out my mace and a sword and impaled the beast. We had killed it!

Charlie Walker (11)

Lakes Primary School, Redcar

The Dungeon Of Doom

I walked around, scanning the surroundings - the dungeon was pitch-black. I heard a twang. Suddenly an arrow shot right past my face! Carrying on, I noticed something emitting light - a torch. I dodged some traps and found... the treasure!

I rushed towards it but I fell down a hole. It was a trap! I had to run quickly because the molten lava was ascending rapidly. I made it out and snatched the treasure but then a door opened and lava came out! I had to run and... I escaped! I stumbled out breathless but suddenly everything went completely black...

Ethan Duthart (10)
Lakes Primary School, Redcar

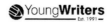

The Lock And Key

I turned around to hear the unusual, creepy whispering coming from the bottom of the well that had been locked up for years. I quickly turned back to my house. The lights started to uncontrollably flicker amongst me as I heard different voices coming from everywhere and they were getting closer.
My parents and sister were out or so I thought. I tried to shout for help but nothing came out. I sprinted into my lounge to stumble upon my family's dead corpses.
Suddenly the wooden door closed all by itself. I knew it was gonna be me next...

Sienna Cannell (10)
Lakes Primary School, Redcar

The Secret Door

Last year, a girl named Sofie discovered something no one had ever discovered before. Sofie went to a forest outside of her house to find she had got lost. But when she went further in her rose gold necklace started flashing. Then all of a sudden a huge metal door appeared in front of Sofie. She put her necklace in the heart-shaped gap and shockingly it fit. The door slowly creaked open, revealing a long dark tunnel.
Sofie decided to enter, not knowing what was about to happen. Sofie walked and walked until she came across... "Aargh!"

Olivia Carlin (11)
Lakes Primary School, Redcar

The Labyrinth

I had until sunset. The guards pushed me in. My heart raced. I thought of how many people or bodies were in the labyrinth.
I took my first step and heard someone call my name. It was my mum! I tried to run to her but she shouted, "Stop!"
I started to lift up. I struggled desperately to figure out what was happening but everything was blurry and I could only hear my mum screaming until I saw it. Thousands of tiny teeth serrated like kitchen knives. I was too weak to escape and within minutes it all went dark.

Matilda Bearpark (10)
Lakes Primary School, Redcar

Getting Out

The tunnel was dark. I couldn't see anything.

Finally, I was out. I entered the labyrinth. There stood the Minotaur. The Minotaur would definitely find me. The darkness made me more scared. I heard the roars of the Minotaur coming from the middle of the maze. When I thought it was all over for me I saw light ahead but I had to make it over there first.

The Minotaur suddenly jumped out from the dark shadows and blocked the exit! How was I going to get out of here? Would I ever see the light of day ever again?

Violet York (11)

Lakes Primary School, Redcar

The Glowing Box

I opened the glowing box... Suddenly there was an icy gust of wind that rushed down the haunted house quickly. I looked inside the box. All there was was an old dusty book. Was this a trick? Then I heard creaking outside the door. What was that? The door swung open. It reached out for the book but I snatched it away just in time. It said, "You don't want to play with that, it's not a toy, you know. Now give it here."
I ran through the corridors. It was coming! I saw the door. It was the exit.

Jessica Leigh Barlow (11)
Lakes Primary School, Redcar

Into The Deep

At the bottom of the ocean with enraged sharks, a torch and the will to live, Jeremiah was at a crossroads: swim up, an easy target for the sharks, or search the ocean floor for a way to escape. So he chose the second option!
He swam up and out a hole in the cage. In the distance, there was a light. Was there someone else there? As Jeremiah and the thing got closer, a gargled scream followed by crunching was heard. Jaws with jagged teeth came into view. It bit his air tank and Jeremiah slowly drowned to death.

Kalvin Powar (10)
Lakes Primary School, Redcar

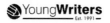

In The Labyrinth

He ran as fast as he could. The monster was right behind him. In just a few more seconds the monster would catch up with him. With his gear slowing him down, the monster jumped on his back. He fell over. Stretching, he reached for his knife. He stabbed the monster in the stomach. At the same time, the monster bit him in the arm. The monster left him on the floor to die. He fought with all his might but the monster was just too strong. Even though John put up a good fight, nobody could beat the Minotaur.

Jack Kenworthy (11)
Lakes Primary School, Redcar

My Near-Death Experience

Suddenly I woke up in a cold dark cave with ticking beside me. Quickly I moved to look around when I saw a colossal bomb and the time was ticking down! I would have just run out the door but it was locked. I had nowhere to go.
All of a sudden I heard someone outside. I banged and screamed on the door until I remembered that I'd learnt how to pick locks but I didn't have very long so I immediately tried.
After many attempts I did it. I quickly grabbed the bomb and threw it into the water.

Lexi Thorpe-Cannon (10)
Lakes Primary School, Redcar

The Ghost House

Just as I reached the door there were strange noises coming from the kitchen. Then there was a scream. I ran until I saw the girl I was looking for. I grabbed her and ran out of the kitchen. We were surrounded by whispers.
All of a sudden she pushed me out the front door. I was home. I was in bed. I thought *it couldn't have been a dream, it felt so real.*
Then there was a knock at the door. It was the girl. She thanked me for saving her. She was trapped in the weird ghost house.

Libby Hammond (10)
Lakes Primary School, Redcar

Superhero James

James gets angry. When he does he gets violent, but this time he figures out he has superpowers. So then he starts launching tables, chairs and starts burning stuff.

He runs out and sees the police chasing a villain so he goes after him and pulls him out of the car and stops the car before it hits anyone. He chases after the villain and catches up so then he jumps on him and takes him to the police. But after, the villain's friends attack James but he arrests them. No one sees James again.

Corey Whitehead (10)
Lakes Primary School, Redcar

Hunted Down

I was being hunted by a killer who had a gun and I was wet, cold and hungry. The dark forest was soggy and muddy. I could hear the footsteps of the killer getting closer. I could see the outline of the killer. I was now starting to get really worried. As I walked through the forest the killer started to shoot me. I started to leg it.
I found a small town. I started to run as fast as I could. The killer shot and killed people around him. Blood was splattered on the walls. My time was up...

Devlin White (10)
Lakes Primary School, Redcar

Hunting For Treasure

Tom took the paper out of the box. A map led to the park. He reached inside a bush at the entrance. Next, Tom was in the centre, up the tree that held the second clue. The last clue was at the lake. It led to an abandoned hut.
Tom looked in the shed. There was a shovel to dig with. There was no way in because it was locked. Tom smashed the window to get in. He found the loose floorboard and dug. He was digging until he hit something hard.
When he was home he opened the chest...

Luke Mosley (10)
Lakes Primary School, Redcar

The Twisted God

I had until sunset, the stars would align and form a beast named Cronoug. I was on a plane to Portugal to steal the malachite. It was twelve at night, I had one day.
I ran to a town and everyone was staring at the top of a statue of Cristiano Ronaldo. It was the malachite! Eleven hours left. I found rope and made a lasso then threw it atop the head. When I began to climb my hands became sweaty and I fell, resulting in a broken ankle. I screamed for someone to grab it quickly.

Junior Dobson (11)
Lakes Primary School, Redcar

Trapped In The Underworld

I woke up in the Underworld. I found a scary beast. It was the Haditaur. Then it tried to kill me. When I ran away it hurt its foot so I helped it. It was lonely so I moved in forever until a hunter came and tried to kill it but I stopped them. We ran away forever. The hunter came back, killed the beast and tried to take me home but the gods brought it back to life and it saved me. We got rid of the hunter because the Haditaur killed the hunter and I got chucked out.

Fahra G (10)
Lakes Primary School, Redcar

The Monster Slayer

I heard a roar of an unknown beast, it came from the cave behind me so I rushed in and lying there was a triple-headed dragon. It was colossal. I couldn't hold back the urge to kill it.
At that moment it woke up. The rage in its eyes stuck me to the spot but I had to get over it. Suddenly in one swift movement, I jumped onto a rock, sword in the air and I leapt right at the beast. But as I was in the air the dragon's mouth opened and I fell in its mouth.

Aiden McClelland (11)
Lakes Primary School, Redcar

YOUNG WRITERS INFORMATION

We hope you have enjoyed reading this book – and that you will continue to in the coming years.

If you're a young writer who enjoys reading and creative writing, or the parent of an enthusiastic poet or story writer, do visit our website **www.youngwriters.co.uk**. Here you will find free competitions, workshops and games, as well as recommended reads, a poetry glossary and our blog. There's lots to keep budding writers motivated to write!

If you would like to order further copies of this book, or any of our other titles, then please give us a call or order via your online account.

Young Writers
Remus House
Coltsfoot Drive
Peterborough
PE2 9BF
(01733) 890066
info@youngwriters.co.uk

Join in the conversation!
Tips, news, giveaways and much more!